Moonlight 🌑 Editions

H.C. Andersen
The Emperor's Nightingale

translated by Erik Haugaard

Schocken Books · New York

First American edition published by Schocken Books 1981
10 9 8 7 6 5 4 3 2 1   81 82 83 84
Text Copyright © 1974 by Erik Christian Haugaard
Illustrations Copyright © 1979 by Editions Gallimard
Published by agreement with Moonlight Publishing Ltd, London

Library of Congress Cataloging in Publication Data
Andersen, H. C. (Hans Christian), 1805–1875. The emperor's nightingale. (Moonlight editions) Translation of Nattergalen. Summary: Though the emperor banishes
the nightingale in preference for a jeweled mechanical imitation, the little bird
remains faithful and returns years later when the emperor is near death and no one
else can help him. [1. Fairy tales. 2. Nightingales—Fiction] I. Haugaard, Erik
    Christian. II. Title. PZ8.A542En 1981   [Fic]   81–40417 AACR2
Manufactured in the United States of America   ISBN 0–8052–3780–1

In China, as you know, the emperor is Chinese, and so are his court and all his people. This story happened a long, long time ago; and that is just the reason why you should hear it now, before it is forgotten. The emperor's palace was the most beautiful in the whole world. It was made of porcelain and had been most costly to build. It was so fragile that you had to be careful not to touch anything and that can be difficult. The gardens were filled with the loveliest flowers; the most beautiful of them had little silver bells that tinkled so you wouldn't pass by without noticing them.

Everything in the emperor's garden was most cunningly arranged. The gardens were so large that even the head gardener did not know exactly how big they were. If you kept walking you finally came to the most beautiful forest, with tall trees that mirrored themselves in deep lakes. The forest stretched all the way to the sea, which was blue and so deep that even large boats could sail so close to the shore that they were shaded by the trees. Here lived a nightingale who sang so sweetly that even the fisherman, who came every night to set his nets, would stop to rest when he heard it, and say: "Blessed God, how beautifully it sings!" But he couldn't listen too long, for he had work to do, and soon he would forget the bird. Yet the next night when he heard it again, he would repeat what he had said the night before: "Blessed God, how beautifully it sings!"

From all over the world travellers came to the emperor's city to admire his palace and gardens; but when they heard the nightingale sing, they all declared that it was the loveliest of all. When they returned to their own countries, they would write long and learned books about the city, the palace, and the garden; but they didn't forget the nightingale. No, that was always mentioned in the very first chapter. Those who could write poetry wrote long odes about the nightingale who lived in the forest, on the shores of the deep blue sea.

These books were read the whole world over; and finally one was also sent to the emperor. He sat down in his golden chair and started to read it. Every once in a while he would nod his head because it pleased him to read how

his own city and his own palace and gardens were praised; but then he came to the sentence: "But the song of the nightingale is the loveliest of all."

"What!" said the emperor. "The nightingale?

I don't know it, I have never heard of it; and yet it lives not only in my empire but in my very garden. That is the sort of thing one can only find out by reading books."

He called his chief courtier, who was so very noble that if anyone of a rank lower than his own, either talked to him, or dared ask him a question, he only answered, "P". And that didn't mean anything at all.

"There is a strange and famous bird called the nightingale," began the emperor. "It is thought to be the most marvellous thing in my empire. Why have I never heard of it?"

"I have never heard of it," answered the courtier. "It has never been presented at court."

"I want it to come this evening and sing for me," demanded the emperor. "The whole world knows of it but I do not."

"I have never heard it mentioned before," said the courtier, and bowed. "But I shall search for it and find it."

But that was more easily said than done. The courtier ran all through the palace, up the stairs and down the stairs, and through the long corridors, but none of the people whom he asked had ever heard of the nightingale. He returned to the emperor and declared that the whole story was nothing but a fable, invented by those people who had written the books. "Your Imperial Majesty should not believe everything that is written. A discovery is one thing and artistic imagination something quite different; it is fiction."

"The book I have just read," replied the emperor, "was sent to me by the great Emperor of Japan; and therefore, every word in it must be the truth. I want to hear the nightingale! And that tonight! If it does not come, then the whole court shall have their stomachs thumped, and that right after they have eaten."

"*Tsing-pe!*" said the courtier. He ran again up and down the stairs and through the corridors; and half the court ran with him, because they didn't want their stomachs thumped! Everywhere they asked about the nightingale that the whole world knew about, and yet no one at court had heard of.

At last they came to the kitchen, where a poor little girl worked, scrubbing the pots and pans. "Oh, I know the nightingale," she said, "I know it well, it sings so beautifully. Every evening I am allowed to bring some leftovers to my poor sick mother who lives down by the sea. Now it is far away, and as I return I often rest in the forest and listen to the nightingale. I get tears in my eyes from it, as

though my mother were kissing me."
"Little kitchenmaid," said the courtier, "I will arrange for a permanent position in the kitchen for you, and permission to see the emperor eat, if you will take us to the

nightingale; it is summoned to court tonight." Half the court went to the forest to find the nightingale. As they were walking along a cow began to bellow.
"Oh!" said all the courtiers. "There it is. What a marvellously powerful voice the little animal has; we have heard it before."

"That is only a cow," said the little kitchen-maid. "We are still far from where the nightingale lives."
They passed a little pond; the frogs were croaking.

"Lovely," sighed the Chinese imperial dean. "I can hear her, she sounds like little church bells ringing."
"No, that is only frogs," said the little kitchenmaid, "but any time now we may hear it."

Just then the nightingale began singing. "There it is!" said the little girl. "Listen. Listen. It is up there on that branch." And she pointed to a little grey bird sitting amid the greenery.

"Is that possible?" exclaimed the chief courtier. "I had not imagined it would look like that. It looks so common! I think it has lost its colour from shyness and out of embarrassment at seeing so many noble people at one time."

"Little nightingale," called the kitchenmaid, "our emperor wants you to sing for him."

"With pleasure," replied the nightingale, and sang as beautifully as he could.

"It sounds like little glass bells," sighed the chief courtier. "Look at its little throat, how it throbs. It is strange that we have never heard of it before; it will be a great success at court."

"Shall I sing another song for the emperor?" asked the nightingale, who thought that the emperor was there.

"Most excellent little nightingale," began the chief courtier, "I have the pleasure to invite you to attend the court tonight, where His Imperial Majesty, the Emperor of China, wishes you to enchant him with your most charming art."

"It sounds best in the green woods," said the nightingale; but when he heard that the emperor insisted, he followed them readily back to the palace.

There every room had been polished and thousands of little golden lamps reflected themselves in the shiny porcelain walls and floors. In the corridors stood all the most beautiful flowers, the ones with silver bells on them; and there was such a draught from all the servants running in and out, and opening and closing doors, that all the bells were tinkling and you couldn't hear what anyone said.

In the grand banquet hall, where the emperor's throne stood, a little golden perch had been hung for the nightingale to sit on. The whole court was there and the little kitchenmaid, who now had the title of Imperial Kitchenmaid, was allowed to stand behind one of the doors and listen. Everyone was dressed in the finest clothes and they all were looking at the little grey bird, towards which the emperor nodded very kindly.

The nightingale's song was so sweet that tears came into the emperor's eyes; and when they ran down his cheeks, the little nightingale sang even more beautifully than it had before. His song spoke to one's heart, and the emperor was so pleased that he ordered his golden slipper to be hung around the little bird's neck. There was no higher honour. But the nightingale thanked him and said that he had been honoured enough already.

"I have seen tears in the eyes of an emperor,

and that is a great enough treasure for me. There is a strange power in an emperor's tears and God knows that is reward enough." Then he sang yet another song.

"That was the most charming and elegant song we have ever heard," said all the ladies of the court. And from that time onward they filled their mouths with water, so they could make a clucking noise, whenever anyone spoke to them, because they thought that then they sounded like the nightingale. Even the chambermaids and the lackeys were satisfied; and that really meant something, for servants are the most difficult to please. Yes, the nightingale was a success.

He was to have his own cage at court, and permission to take a walk twice a day and once during the night. Twelve servants were to accompany him; each held on tightly to a silk ribbon that was attached to the poor bird's legs. There wasn't any pleasure in such an outing.

The whole town talked about the marvellous bird. Whenever two people met in the street they would sigh; one would say, "night," and the other, "gale"; and then they would understand each other perfectly. Twelve delicatessen shop owners named their children "Nightingale," but not one of them could sing.

One day a package arrived for the emperor;

on it was written: "Nightingale."

"It is probably another book about our famous bird," said the emperor. But he was wrong; it was a mechanical nightingale. It lay in a little box and was supposed to look like the real one, though it was made of silver and gold and studded with sapphires, diamonds,

and rubies. When you wound it up, it could sing one of the songs the real nightingale sang; and while it performed its little silver tail would go up and down. Around its neck hung a ribbon on which was written: "The Emperor of Japan's nightingale is inferior to the Emperor of China's."

"It is beautiful!" exclaimed the whole court. And the messenger who had brought it had the title of Supreme Imperial Nightingale Deliverer bestowed upon him at once.

"They ought to sing together, it will be a duet," said everyone, and they did. But that didn't work out well at all; for the real bird sang in his own manner and the mechanical one had a cylinder inside its chest instead of a heart. "It is not its fault," said the imperial music master. "It keeps perfect time, it belongs to my school of music." Then the mechanical nightingale had to sing solo. Everyone agreed that its song was just as beautiful as the real nightingale's; and besides, the artificial bird was much pleasanter to look at, with its sapphires, rubies, and diamonds that glittered like bracelets and brooches.

The mechanical nightingale sang its song

thirty-three times and did not grow tired. The court would have liked to hear it the thirty-fourth time, but the emperor thought that the real nightingale ought to sing now. But where was it? Nobody had noticed that he had flown out through an open window, to

his beloved green forest.

"What is the meaning of this!" said the emperor angrily, and the whole court blamed the nightingale and called him an ungrateful creature.

"But the best bird remains," they said, and the

mechanical bird sang its song once more. It was the same song, for it knew no other; but it was very intricate, so the courtiers didn't know it by heart yet. The imperial music master praised the bird and declared that it was better than the real nightingale, not only on the outside where the diamonds were, but also inside.

"Your Imperial Majesty and gentlemen; you understand that the real nightingale cannot be depended upon. One never knows what he will sing; whereas, in the mechanical bird, everything is determined. There is one song and no other! One can explain everything. We can open it up to examine and appreciate how human thought has fashioned the wheels and the cylinder, and put them where they are to turn just as they should."

"Precisely what I was thinking!" said the whole court in a chorus. And the imperial music master was given permission to show the new nightingale to the people on the following Sunday.

The emperor thought that they, too, should hear the bird. They did and they were as delighted as if they had got drunk on too much tea. It was all very Chinese. They pointed with their licking fingers toward heaven, nodded, and said: "Oh!"

But the poor fisherman, who had heard the real nightingale, mumbled, "It sounds

beautiful and like the bird's song, but something is missing, though I don't know what it is."

The real nightingale was banished from the empire.

The mechanical bird was given a silk pillow to rest upon, close to the emperor's bed; and all the presents it had received were piled around it. Among them were both gold and precious stones. Its title was Supreme Imperial Night-table Singer and its rank was Number One to the Left.—The emperor thought the left side was more distinguished because that is the side where the heart is, even in an emperor.

The imperial music master wrote a work in twenty-five volumes about the mechanical nightingale. It was not only long and learned but filled with the most difficult Chinese words, so everyone bought it and said they had read and understood it, for otherwise they would have been considered stupid and had to have their stomachs poked.

A whole year went by. The emperor, the court, and all the Chinese in China knew every note of the supreme imperial night-table singer's song by heart; but that was the very reason why they liked it so much: they could sing it themselves, and they did. The street urchins sang: "Zi-zi-zizzi, cluck-cluck-cluck-cluck." And so did the emperor. Oh, it was delightful!

But one evening, when the bird was singing

its very best and the emperor was lying in bed listening to it, something said: "Clang," inside it. It was broken! All the wheels whirred around and then the bird was still.

The emperor jumped out of bed and called his physician but he couldn't do anything, so the imperial watchmaker was fetched. After a great deal of talking and tinkering he repaired the bird, but he declared that the cylinders were worn and new ones could not be fitted. The bird would have to be spared; it could not be played so often.

It was a catastrophe. Only once a year was the mechanical bird allowed to sing, and then it had difficulty finishing its song. But the imperial music master made a speech wherein he explained, using the most difficult words, that the bird was as good as ever; and then it was.

Five years passed and a great misfortune happened. Although everyone loved the old emperor, he had fallen ill; and they all agreed that he would not get well again. It was said that a new emperor had already been chosen; and when people in the street asked the chief courtier how the emperor was, he would

shake his head and say: "P".

Pale and cold, the emperor lay in his golden bed. The whole court believed him to be already dead and they were busy visiting and paying their respects to the new emperor. The lackeys were all out in the street gossiping, and the chambermaids were drinking coffee. All the floors in the whole palace were covered with black carpets so that no one's steps would disturb the dying emperor; and that's why it was as quiet as quiet could be in the whole palace.

But the emperor was not dead yet. Pale and motionless he lay in his great golden bed; the long velvet curtains were drawn, and the golden tassels moved slowly in the wind, for one of the windows was open. The moon shone down upon the emperor, and its light was reflected in the diamonds of the mechanical bird.

The emperor could hardly breathe; he felt as though someone were sitting on his chest. He opened his eyes. Death was sitting there. He was wearing the emperor's golden crown and held his gold sabre in one hand and his imperial banner in the other. From the folds of the curtains that hung around his bed, strange faces looked down at the emperor. Some of them were frighteningly ugly, and others mild and kind. They were the evil and good deeds that the emperor had done. Now, while Death was sitting on his heart, they

were looking down at him.

"Do you remember?" whispered first one and then another. And they told him things that made the cold sweat of fear appear on his forehead.

"No, no I don't remember! It is not true!"

shouted the emperor. "Music, music, play the great Chinese gong," he begged, "so that I will not be able to hear what they are saying." But the faces kept talking and Death, like a real Chinese, nodded his head to every word that was said.

"Little golden nightingale, sing!" demanded the emperor. "I have given you gold and precious jewels and with my own hands have I hung my golden slipper around your neck. Sing! Please sing!"

But the mechanical nightingale stood as still as ever, for there was no one to wind it up; and then, it couldn't sing.

Death kept staring at the emperor out of the empty sockets in his skull; and the palace was still, so terrifyingly still.

All at once the most beautiful song broke the silence. It was the nightingale, who had heard of the emperor's illness and torment. He sat on a branch outside his window and sang to bring him comfort and hope. As he sang, the faces in the folds of the curtains faded and the blood pulsed with greater force through the emperor's weak body. Death himself listened and said, "Please, little nightingale, sing on!"

"Will you give me the golden sabre? Will you give me the imperial banner? Will you give me the golden crown?"
Death gave each of his trophies for a song; and then the nightingale sang about the quiet

churchyard, where white roses grow, where fragrant elderberrry trees are, and where the grass is green from the tears of those who come to mourn. Death longed so much for his garden that he flew out of the window, like a white cold mist.
"Thank you, thank you," whispered the

emperor, "you heavenly little bird, I remember you. You have I banished from my empire and yet you came to sing for me; and when you sang the evil phantoms that taunted me disappeared, and Death himself left my heart. How shall I reward you?"

"You have rewarded me already," said the nightingale. "I shall never forget that, the first time I sang for you, you gave me the tears from your eyes; and to a poet's heart, those are jewels. But sleep so you can become well and strong; I shall sing for you."

The little grey bird sang; and the emperor slept, so blessedly, so peacefully.

The sun was shining in through the window when he woke; he did not feel ill any more. None of his servants had come, for they thought that he was already dead; but the nightingale was still there and he was singing.

"You must come always," declared the emperor. "I shall only ask you to sing when you want to. And the mechanical bird I shall break in a thousand pieces."

"Don't do that," replied the nightingale. "The mechanical bird sang as well as it could, keep it. I can't build my nest in the palace; let me come to visit you when I want to, and I shall sit on the branch outside your window and sing for you. And my song shall make you happy and make you thoughtful. I shall sing not only of those who are happy but also of those who suffer. I shall sing of the good and of the evil that happen around you, and yet are hidden from you. For a little songbird flies far. I visit the poor fisherman's cottage and the peasant's hut, far away from your palace and your court. I love your heart more than your crown, and yet I feel that the crown has a fragrance of something holy about it. I will come! I will sing for you! Only one thing must you promise me."

"I will promise you anything," said the emperor, who had dressed himself in his imperial clothes and was holding his golden sabre, pressing it against his heart.

"I beg of you never tell anyone that you have a little bird that tells you everything, for then you will fare even better." And with those words the nightingale flew away.

The servants entered the room to look at their dead master. There they stood gaping when the emperor said: "Good morning."